TREASURY OF
AESOP'S FABLES

This book belongs to

....

TREASURY OF AESOP'S FABLES

Illustrated and retold
by Val Biro

AWARD PUBLICATIONS LIMITED

ISBN 978-1-84135-506-1

Illustrations copyright © Val Biro
Text copyright © Award Publications Limited
This edition copyright © 2007

First published 2007

Published by Award Publications Limited,
The Old Riding School, The Welbeck Estate,
Worksop, Nottinghamshire, S80 3LR

www.awardpublications.co.uk

10 3

Printed in Malaysia

CONTENTS

The Donkey
and the Lapdog

Once there was a man who had a house and a farm. The house was filled with nice tables and chairs and the farm produced lots of lovely things to eat. The man was very proud of his house and farm.

He also had a donkey and a lapdog. Both animals had four legs, but otherwise they were very different.

The donkey worked hard all day on the farm. He was very good at it. He always had plenty of food and he slept in the stable at night.

It was a warm and comfortable stable, but the donkey kept thinking about the lapdog.

"I cart and carry all day long," he said to himself, "while that silly dog has an easy life with everybody making a fuss of him!"

This was perfectly true because the lapdog played all day in the house, and he was very good at it. So good, in fact, that everybody fussed over and petted him and he didn't do a stroke of work.

He just enjoyed himself all day and he slept
in a soft bed at night, a real doggy bed, right by
the side of his master.

At mealtimes he would do what he could
do best of all; he would sit on people's laps.
That's why he was called a lapdog. He sat on
his master's lap at dinner, and he had lovely
things to eat. What a lucky dog!

The donkey looked through the window and he was very jealous.

"That dog must be very clever," he thought, "to have all that fussing and petting and all that lovely food without having to do any work for it."

The donkey said, "I wish I could be more like the dog. The farmer and his wife would make a pet of me and I would do nothing but play all day."

So one day he trotted into the house and began to play just like the dog.

He jumped and capered around the room, but
he upset the table and chairs. He was far too
big and clumsy. Soon the room was a mess.

"Never mind!" the donkey thought and he
tried to bark just like the little lapdog, but all
he could say was "HEE-HAW!"

Then he saw the lovely things to eat. He
jumped up on his master's lap, just like the dog.
"That should do the trick," thought
the donkey.

"Now my master will fuss over me and pet me and give me lovely food for being such a good lapdog."

But not a bit of it. The master was very angry. He jumped up, shouting, "You clumsy brute! What do you think you are doing? You're a donkey, not a lapdog!"

He grabbed a broom and chased the donkey
back to the stable. The master's wife ran after the
donkey and the master, shaking her rolling-pin, and
the lapdog ran after them all!

"HEE-HAW, HEE-HAW!" brayed the
donkey as he ran back to his stable.

The donkey decided he had been silly to
pretend to be a lapdog. Lapdogs were silly and
useless. It was better to be a donkey, doing
donkey work, eating donkey food, and sleeping
in a donkey stable.

"I am no good at being a lapdog," said the donkey. "I will just be a donkey." And he has been a donkey ever since, which is what he had been best at being all along.

The Lion
and the Mouse

Once a lion caught a mouse. He wanted to eat it.

"This mouse is so small it will never make me a meal," said the lion, "but I might as well gobble it up."

"Please let me go!" cried the mouse.
"Be kind to me and one day I will help you."
That was a funny thing to say because how could a tiny mouse ever help a big strong lion? It sounded ridiculous!

The lion laughed. "How could a little mouse ever help me?" But he let the mouse go because the mouse was brave enough to speak to him. Besides, the lion wasn't very hungry anyway. The mouse squeaked his thanks and scampered away.

Soon after, the lion was caught in a net. He
had been hunting in the forest because by then
he really was hungry. He did not know that
some men, who were also out hunting, had set
a trap for him. He roared with anger. It was a
frightening sound. All the animals in the forest
ran away from the terrible noise, except one.

The mouse heard the lion's roar and ran to help.

He knew that the lion was in trouble, and he remembered the promise he had made when the lion had let him go.

The mouse saw that the lion was caught in a net made of strong ropes. With his sharp little teeth the mouse bit through the net. It was hard work and took a long time but the mouse went on nibbling until at last he made a big hole in the net.

The lion was free! He climbed out of the
trap and smiled his thanks at the mouse.

The mouse sat down and smiled back at
the lion. You see, a mouse *can* help a lion!

And from that day on the mouse and the
lion were the best of friends.

The Fox and
the Stork

Fox and Stork were good friends and they often spent their days together. There was only one problem – Fox was always playing tricks on Stork.

One day Fox asked Stork to dinner. He wanted to play a trick on her. "This will be one of my best," he thought.

When Stork arrived, he politely showed her into the house. The steaming hot soup was already served, and it smelled delicious. But Fox had played a trick! He put the soup in two bowls but did not lay out any spoons, and he knew Stork would be too polite to ask for one.

When they sat down, Fox began to eat straight away, lapping up the soup with his long tongue. He cleaned his bowl in no time. But Stork could not drink the soup because of her long beak. How Fox laughed! Poor Stork went home hungry, while Fox lapped up her soup as well.

Now Stork was angry. The time had come for sly Fox to be taught a lesson. She sat down to work out a plan.

"Aha!" she finally said with glee, "I know how to pay him back!" and she went about making her preparations.

Soon after she asked Fox if he would come to dinner.

Fox arrived at the arranged time. There was
the most delicious smell of meat in the air and
he could hardly wait. Stork put the meat in two
jugs with long necks. When Fox sat down, he
stared at the table in dismay. There in front of
him was Stork's trick.

Clever Stork! She knew perfectly well that Fox would never get his big nose down the neck of the narrow jug, and he would be too polite to pick it up and tip the meat into his mouth.

Now it was Fox who could not eat!

Fox just sat there, glaring at Stork as she delicately picked out the meat with her long beak. Soon she had finished her own meal, and then she pulled her guest's jug towards her and ate his as well. So Stork finished both dinners, and Fox went home hungry.

And since then, Fox has always thought twice before playing tricks on Stork.

The Man, His
Son and the Ass

A man and his son were going to town. They wanted to sell their ass and, to make sure that he looked fit and well, they decided to walk behind him.

Riding him would have made the ass tired, so they walked one behind the other. Their ass was walking in front of them.

They met some old women standing by the roadside. "Look at that!" they said. "What a thoughtless man to let his poor son trudge along the dusty road when there is a perfectly good ass to ride on. Let your poor son ride!" said the old women.

The man thought it would please the old
women if he did what they told him. Otherwise
they might think he was thoughtless.

So the son rode on the ass and the man
walked in front. The man was well pleased to
have taken such good advice.

Soon they met some old men sitting by the roadside.

"Look at that!" they said. "What a selfish boy! There he is riding on the ass while his old father is trudging along the dusty road."

The old men said, "Let your poor father ride!"

The son thought that it might please the old men if he did what they told him, otherwise they might think he was selfish.

So the man rode on the ass and the son walked in front. The son was well pleased to have taken such good advice.

After a while they met some workmen by
the roadside.

"Look at that!" said the workmen, laughing.
"What a crazy pair! An ass is made for two
people to ride on, yet the boy is trudging along
the dusty road. You should both ride on that
ass!" said the workmen.

The man thought it would please the workmen if he did what they said. Otherwise they might think he was crazy. So the man and his son both rode on the ass.

Soon, the ass grew tired under the double weight and stumbled from time to time as he trudged along.

Some children were playing by the roadside.

"Look at that!" they said. "What cruel
people! They are both riding on that poor ass
who keeps stumbling along. It should be the
other way round! Let the poor ass ride!" said
the children.

"How ever could an ass ride?" wondered the man. But he thought he should please the children, so he decided that somehow he and his son would have to carry the ass. They got off, and the only way the man could think of was to tie the ass's legs together over a pole. So the man and his son carried the ass on a pole.

When they came to the town, everybody
laughed at them. "Look at that!" they cried.
"Have you ever seen anything like it? They
must be quite mad, to carry an ass on a pole!"

The ass did not like this and he kicked at the pole. He hated all that noise and was tired of hanging upside down. The man and his son were just crossing a bridge over a river when the ass started to kick.

He kicked so hard that the pole broke and
the ass fell into the river.

Splash!

And the man and his son fell into the river, too. *Splash! Splash!*

What a calamity – all three splashing helplessly about in the water. And all because the man and his son had tried too hard to please everyone, and in the end had pleased no one!

The Monkey and the Fishermen

Once there was a monkey who lived in
the trees. Most monkeys do, because
they like swinging from branch to branch.
This monkey had swung his way through
every tree in the jungle.

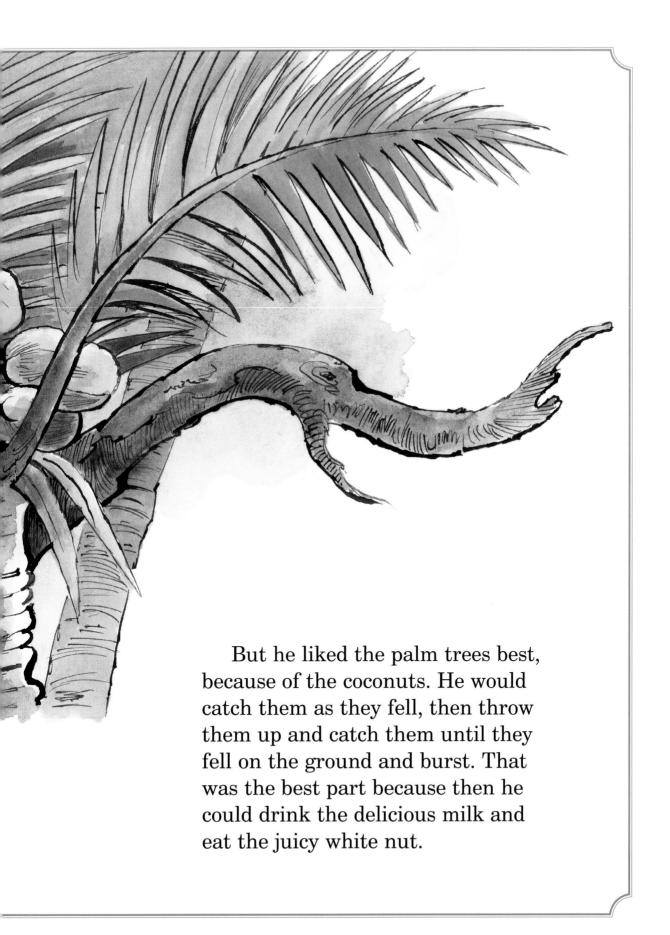

But he liked the palm trees best, because of the coconuts. He would catch them as they fell, then throw them up and catch them until they fell on the ground and burst. That was the best part because then he could drink the delicious milk and eat the juicy white nut.

One day he looked into the river below the tree. He saw the fish swimming about and poking their noses into the air. He thought it would be nice to have some fish for supper.

"I wish I could catch some fish," he said,
"but I don't know how. They don't fall off trees
like coconuts do."

Just then two fishermen came along the
riverbank. They were carrying a big net
between them.

"Now, that is interesting. I wonder what
they're going to do with a net?" thought
the monkey.

"Perhaps it's for playing a game, like
football or tennis?" The monkey watched
carefully to see what would happen next.

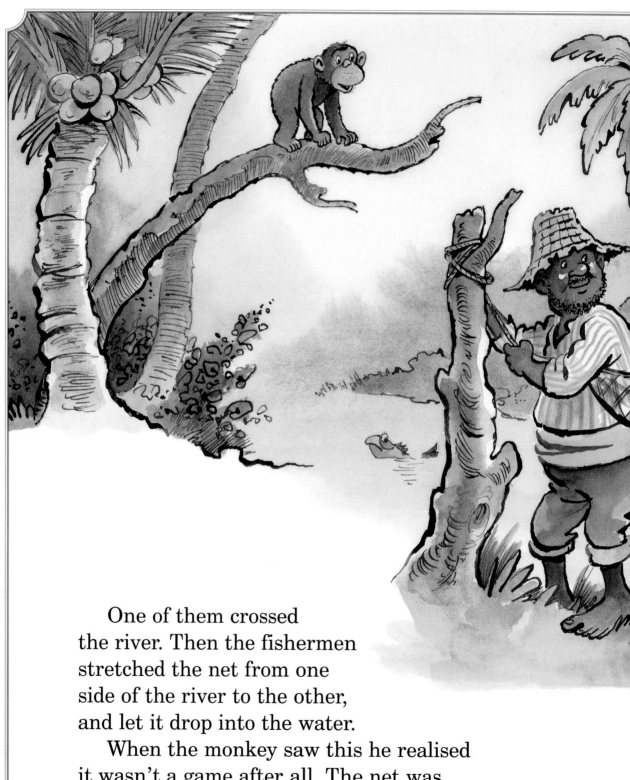

One of them crossed
the river. Then the fishermen
stretched the net from one
side of the river to the other,
and let it drop into the water.

When the monkey saw this he realised
it wasn't a game after all. The net was
for catching the fish. What a good idea!

The fisherman who had
crossed the river came back to
his friend.

"We should catch lots of
fish," they said, and went off to
wait in a shady spot round the
bend of the river.

At last the monkey knew about fishing.

"I shall try it for myself," he said, jumping
down from the tree. "Why didn't I think of it
before? All I need is a net, and then I shall
have all the fish I want for my supper!" And off
he went to find a net.

He knew of an old hut nearby and ran to see
what he could find there. Soon he found an old
net and dragged it down to the river. It was
very heavy, but he didn't mind as he was too
excited about fishing and a fishy dinner.

When he got back to his tree, he tried to do
the same as the fishermen had done. He tied
one end of the net to a large branch, then
jumped into the water with the net.

Poor monkey! He couldn't swim. The net wrapped itself round his arms and legs and he struggled to get free, but he got so tangled up that he nearly drowned.

Just then the fishermen came back. "Look!"
said one of them. "There is a big furry fish
caught in the net! Did you ever see one like it?"

They laughed to see the silly monkey, but
they pulled him out of the river.

"Just remember," said one of them to the
monkey, "there's more to catching fish than
you think. You must learn about it first, before
you try."

Then the fishermen walked off to see to
their own net.

Realising that what the fishermen said
was true, the monkey ran back to his tree.
"I am no good at catching fish," he said.
"I will just catch the coconuts!"
And from that day on, he has never
been fishing again!

The Ass
in the Pond

An ass had a big load of salt on his back. He was walking home from market behind the farmer who carried nothing but a stick and whistled happily as he walked.

The ass was miserable. He was hot and
thirsty and it was difficult to walk because his
load was so heavy. But he plodded on, groaning
under the weight and slipping and tripping on
the rough and dusty road.

The road was getting rougher and dustier
and the ass kept slipping more and more
until, suddenly, there was a disaster.
He slipped and fell into the
pond. *Splash!*

"My salt! My salt!" cried the farmer in
alarm, knowing what would happen to his
precious salt if it got wet. He tried to pull it
out but the water washed away all the salt.

The ass wasn't worried at all. He enjoyed the nice cool water. When the ass got out his load was much lighter because now the sacks on his back were almost empty.

Now it was the ass who felt cool and light and happy, and the farmer, who had lost all his salt, felt hot and bothered and miserable.

The next day the ass had a big load of sponges on his back. The farmer had taken him to market again and they were walking back along the same road. It was even hotter and the ass felt most unhappy under his load.

He saw the pond a little way ahead and remembered how much cooler he had felt the day before, after he had fallen in, and how much lighter his load had become.

"I shall try it again," he said to himself.

So he fell into the pond on purpose to make the load lighter. But this time the farmer was not alarmed at all.

"Oho, my friend! I know what you're up to!" he said with a grin. "So you thought that the sponges would be washed away like the salt? Well, climb out and see!"

The ass had no idea what the farmer was talking about. He felt much cooler after his soaking, and when he climbed out he expected that his load would be much lighter, too. But the sponges filled up with water and the load was much heavier.

No wonder the farmer had a broad grin on his face, and the ass was scowling miserably. Silly ass!

The Sick Lion

It was a hot day. Lion felt too tired to hunt for his dinner. He was getting old and hunting was becoming more and more difficult, especially on a day like this. But he was hungry, so he sat down and began to think.

"How can I look for my dinner without all that running about?" he asked himself. He spent a while deep in thought, and suddenly he had an idea. Lion grinned a very wicked grin.

"I know," he said. "My dinner can come
to me."

He went into his den and when he came out
again he was wearing his pyjamas. Soon all
the animals in the forest came to see what
was wrong with Lion. They were careful not
to get too close to him because lions are
dangerous animals.

Lion began to limp. Then he began to shiver, and then he mopped his brow. When he was sure that all the animals were watching him, he turned away. He pretended to be sick and went to bed in his den.

The other animals felt sorry for him.
"We must go and visit him," they said. They
thought that a sick lion would not be so
dangerous. But clever Fox had spied on Lion
and seen him grin his wicked grin.

"Take care," warned Fox. "He might eat you."

"Perhaps he's right. Maybe we should not visit Lion," said the others. Rabbit, who was the most timid of all, scampered away and some of the others ran after him.

But Cow was very brave. "You are such cowards," she said. "Poor Lion is sick and I want to cheer him up."

So she went first and knocked at the den door. "Come in, come in!" called Lion from his bed. He made his voice sound feeble, and the darkness hid his wicked grin.

So Cow went in, but she never came out.
All the other animals said how brave Cow was,
and did not notice that she never came out of
the den.

The next day Pig said, "I will copy Cow and show that I am brave," and he followed Cow's footprints into Lion's den.

The others saw Pig go in through the den door, leaving his own footprints in the sand. The rest of the animals wondered who else would be as brave as Pig.

Goat went in next, to copy Pig. But neither
Goat nor Pig came out again. Only their
footprints remained in the sand.

Rabbit and Duck were still afraid to go into
Lion's den but Rabbit said, "I am not really a
coward. I will copy Goat and go in, but I will
wait until tomorrow."

The next day, Rabbit went
into the den to copy Goat,
and Duck waddled after
to copy Rabbit. Nobody
saw them again.

Clever Fox was watching everything from a distance. He had seen all the animals go into the den to cheer up the sick lion.

"Lion must be feeling very cheerful by now," he thought, "with all his dinners walking in like that."

Fox stood by the door and called, "How are you, Lion?" Lion was delighted to hear the voice of another visitor. He licked his lips and grinned his wicked grin, but he made his voice sound very feeble.

"Very poorly," said Lion. "Why don't you come in, my friend?" Lion hoped that Fox would copy all the other animals and come in to be eaten, but Fox was too clever for that. He stood by the door and looked at the footprints in the sand.

Fox said, "Because I am not a copycat!
I see all these footprints going in, but none
coming OUT!"

Fox was too clever to follow all the other
animals into the den to be eaten by the lion,
and he went away.

So Lion had no dinner that day.

The Hare and
the Tortoise

Once there was a hare who could run very
fast and a tortoise who could only go very
slowly – plod, plod, plod.

One day they met in a meadow.

"I can run much faster than you," said the
hare to the tortoise.

"Maybe you can," said the tortoise. He was
tired of being teased about being slow, but he
knew one day he would teach the boastful hare
a lesson. "Let's have a race and see," he said.

"How could a plodding tortoise win a race
against me?" said the hare, laughing.

All the animals came to watch the race.
They put up a starting line and a finishing post
and told the hare and the tortoise to stand side
by side on the starting line.

The fox called out, "Ready, steady, go!"

The hare ran fast – hop, hop, hop – for he was the fastest animal in the forest. He ran so fast that he was soon out of sight.

The tortoise crawled slowly – plod, plod, plod – for he was the slowest animal in the forest.

The hare was so far ahead that when he
looked round he could not see the tortoise
at all.

"He will never catch up with me," he
thought.

It was a hot day and the hare came to a big
shady tree. "I have lots of time," said the hare.
He stopped for a rest and lay down to sleep –
snore, snore, snore.

Meanwhile, the tortoise plodded on steadily. When he came to the big shady tree he saw the hare fast asleep.

"I must keep going," said the tortoise and on he crawled – plod, plod, plod. He didn't stop or look round and soon he saw the finishing post ahead.

At last the hare woke up, but it was too late. He jumped up and ran as fast as he could to the finishing post. When he got there he saw the tortoise crawling past the post with a big smile on his face.

The tortoise had won the race. All the animals were cheering.

"I hope you've learned a lesson," said the tortoise to the hare. "Slow and steady wins the race."

The Bear and
the Travellers

One day, two friends were travelling
together on a lonely road. The road led
into a big, dark wood near the tall mountains
in India. The two friends were completely alone
in the silent wood. They were silent, too, as
they walked along.

One of them was young and the other was old. At last the young man spoke.

"I don't like this place. It feels dangerous. But never mind. We are good friends and if we stick close together, nothing can hurt us."

The old man agreed with his friend and they continued on their journey.

Suddenly a brown bear came out of the woods. He was huge and fierce. He looked straight at the two travellers, with a wicked grin on his face.

"Ah-ha!" he growled. "Here comes my dinner!"
He grinned even more, showing his big, sharp
teeth, and began lumbering towards the two
travellers.

The men were afraid and ran away. They had no guns and the old man was too weak to fight the bear with his stick.

The young man was stronger, but he was so frightened that he ran for his life.

The bear chased after them. His big paws churned up the dust and as he drew nearer and nearer.

The old man knew that he could not run fast enough to get away from the bear, so he called out to his young friend, "Take my stick and fight the bear!"

But the young man ran fast and climbed up a tall tree to hide. He was safe.

The old man was slow and could not climb. Then the old man suddenly remembered that people said a bear will not touch someone who is dead.

So he lay down and pretended to be dead.
He hoped that what people had said about
bears was right, because he knew his friend
was not going to help him.

The big brown bear came up and walked all around him. "At least I have half my dinner!" the bear said.

The bear sniffed the old man's feet, then his legs and then his back.

The old man stayed very, very still. He shut his eyes tight and held his breath.

The bear thought that there was something wrong, so he went on sniffing. He sniffed the old man's hands, his head and his nose.

Then the bear
sniffed at his ear.

"He must be dead," the bear growled. "I
never eat dead people." The bear was very
cross. Half his dinner was up in a tree where
he could not reach it, and the other half lay
dead in front of him.

So the bear went away without his dinner.
"I am certainly out of luck today," he thought.
The old man opened his eyes and saw the bear
disappearing into the big dark wood, but he lay
very still until it was gone.

When it was safe, the young man in the tree
came down. He had seen everything from his
hiding place and he wanted to know why the
bear had gone away without eating his friend.

He had also seen the bear mutter something
before it went away.

"What did the bear say when he sniffed at
your ear?" the young man asked his friend.

The old man sat up and got to his feet. He
looked sternly at the young man.

"That I should never again travel with a friend who leaves me in danger!" said the old man.

Then he turned, and as he walked away he said, "Remember, a true friend will never let you down."

The Ducks and
the Tortoise

A tortoise was tired of crawling. All he ever seemed to do was crawl. The house on his back was big and heavy and his four stumpy legs were short and weak.

Walking made him very tired and running was quite impossible, so he crawled everywhere very slowly.

He could swim, but that became a little boring after a while, being underwater when what he really wanted was to see the great big world above.

"I wish I could fly like the ducks!" he said. When the ducks landed nearby he crawled over to them. "Will you teach me to fly?" he asked.

"You can't fly without wings," said the ducks. "Anyway, you are quite the wrong shape with that big round house on your back and those short stubby legs. You would look ridiculous."

But the tortoise begged and pleaded with the ducks.

After a while the ducks got tired of this silly,
pestering tortoise and decided to teach him
a lesson.

"You can't fly up into the sky just like that,"
said one of them. "But we can take you up on
this stick. Hold it in your mouth."

The ducks took hold of the stick at each end and the tortoise grabbed it in the middle. Then the ducks spread their wings and up they all flew.

They flew over a village. The people were amazed to see a tortoise in the air. Who had ever seen such a thing?

It was such a strange sight that they stared and waved their arms. The tortoise saw the people waving and it made him very proud.

"They must think that I am a very clever tortoise," he thought. Yes, he was the only tortoise in the world who could fly, and he had to tell them.

"Look, I can fly!" the tortoise shouted, opening his mouth – which was not a very clever thing to do!

When the tortoise opened his mouth, he let go of the stick and down he fell. *Thump!*

That's the end of the story, except that the tortoise decided that flying wasn't such a good thing after all – at least not for tortoises!

The Boy Who Cried Wolf

A boy lay in a field all day, looking after his
sheep. He lay in the hot sun and the sheep
grazed around him in peace. There was nothing
much to do until nightfall, when he would take
his flock down to the village, except to keep a
look-out for any hungry wolves.

He was very bored, so he decided to play a
trick on the villagers. If he shouted for help,
as they had told him to do if he ever saw a wolf,
they would soon come running to help him
chase it away.

He jumped up and ran to the edge of the field, shouting, "Wolf! Wolf!"

The men in the village below came running to help chase the wolf away.

The boy thought it was very funny to see the old men come racing to help him, banging their shields and waving their hoes and flails, and shouting to frighten the wolf away.

The men looked everywhere, but there was
no wolf. They went home after counting the
sheep to make sure none were missing.

They decided they must have frightened the wolf away with all their noise.

The boy laughed. He thought he was very clever to play such a trick on the villagers.

The next day the boy played the same trick.
"Wolf! Help! The wolf is eating my sheep," he
cried as he ran down the hill towards the village.

Again the men came running to help chase
the wolf away. They thought he would be very
hungry by now, so they ran even faster and
made even more noise.

The boy laughed and laughed as he watched
the men rush up, puffing and panting, shouting
and yelling to frighten away the wolf. But there
was no wolf!

When the men saw the boy laughing, they realised he had tricked them. "Be careful, boy," they said to him. "You will cry 'Wolf!' once too often." But the boy just laughed at them.

One day a real wolf came into the field – a real, live, hungry wolf, who hadn't eaten for days. He saw the sheep grazing nearby and sprang at them. Up jumped the boy.

"Wolf! Wolf!" he cried as he ran away.
He had never seen such a big wolf before, and
he could do nothing to protect his sheep, except
shout for help. He ran as fast as he could to the
edge of the field, waving his arms.

But this time the men did not come.

They heard the boy clearly enough, shouting and crying, "Wolf! A real wolf has come!" but the men took no notice and carried on talking to each other.

The boy could not convince them that there
was a real wolf this time. They just laughed
at him.

"He is only playing a trick on us again,"
they said to each other. So the boy gave up and
went away.

So when the boy came back to the field,
he found that the wolf had eaten all his sheep.
There was not one of them left and the wolf
had gone, too.

The boy sat down. He knew that it was all
his own fault. He had tricked the men before
with his lies and no one goes on believing a
liar – even when they are telling the truth!

The Goose
That Laid the
Golden Eggs

A man and his wife had a goose. They lived in a cottage and the goose lived in the yard. The man and his wife were poor. They grumbled all day and wished all the time to be rich.

"I wish we had a bigger house," said the man, sighing.

His wife agreed. "I wish I had some sparkling jewels," she said.

The man sighed again. "And I wish I had a bag of gold," he said.

One day the goose laid a golden egg. It lay
on the ground sparkling and glittering.

"Look at that," called his wife. The man
could hardly believe his eyes. He snatched up
the egg. It was smooth and large and heavy.

"It's solid gold!" he shouted.

"It's worth a fortune!" cried his wife.
They danced round and round in excitement.

"We shall be rich!" they shouted. And they
danced around again thinking of bags of gold
and piles of jewels, until they were quite
exhausted.

The man and his wife could hardly wait
until market day to sell the egg and buy all the
things they wanted.

Then the goose laid another golden egg.

"Just think," said the wife. "If our goose
goes on laying golden eggs day after day, we
shall soon be the richest people in the village."

But the man did not reply because he was
thinking very hard. "It will take a long time for
us to become very rich with only one egg a
day," he thought.

"I want to be rich now," he said.

"So do I," said his wife. "But what shall we do?"

"The goose must be full of gold," said the man. "If I cut it open now, we shall have all the gold at once!"

"You are right!" his wife replied. "The goose must be made of gold! I can't wait! Let's cut her open and see."

So the man went and fetched a carving knife. They cut the goose open. The man looked inside one half and his wife looked inside the other. They looked at each other and then looked inside the goose again. They could not believe their eyes.

They had expected the goose to be full of gold, but the goose was full of goose!

They had killed the goose for nothing! So the man and his wife had no more golden eggs, and no more goose! They were the silliest people in the village, because they had killed the goose that laid the golden eggs.

The Eagle
and the Man

Once an eagle was caught in a net. Poor eagle! He flapped his great wings and tore at the net with his beak, but it was no good. The net was too strong and he could not free himself.

The eagle knew that if he could not get free from the net he would die.

Just then a man saw the eagle in the net.

"What a beautiful creature!" he said. "The king of the birds!" But then he saw that the eagle was caught in a net and the man knew what he had to do.

He climbed up to the great bird and set it free. So the man saved the eagle's life. The grateful eagle flew off.

The eagle decided that he would repay the man's kindness if he could.

One day the man went to sleep near a very old wall. The eagle saw him lying in the shade and his sharp eyes told him that the crumbling wall was so old that it might fall down at any minute.

There was no time to lose! The man was fast asleep, so the eagle flew down and snatched his hat away. He took it in his talons and, with a flapping of his great wings, he flew away.

The man looked up and saw what had happened.

"Give it back!" the man shouted. "That's my hat!"

He ran after the eagle. He ran fast, but the eagle flew even faster. The man recognised the eagle as the one he had saved, but he could not think why he should have stolen the hat.

After a while the eagle dropped the hat and flew away. The man picked up the hat and saw that it was not damaged.

The man went back to the wall. He was still puzzled about why the eagle had taken his hat but he wanted to finish his sleep.

But when he got back the man was amazed to find that the old wall had fallen down! It would certainly have killed him. So the eagle had saved the man's life.

The man looked up and saw the great bird circling in the sky. "Thank you, my friend," he called to the eagle.

The Town Mouse
and the
Country Mouse

A poor country mouse lived in a ditch. It was just an ordinary ditch, but he had made it quite comfortable.

He enjoyed the peace of the countryside all around him, because he was just an ordinary country mouse.

One day he wrote to the rich town mouse and asked him to dinner. It would be nice to see his old friend again, he thought, and he was sure the town mouse would enjoy the peace and quiet of the countryside. So he tidied up the ditch, prepared a dinner and waited for his friend to arrive.

The town mouse came. He was
very rich and dressed in expensive clothes.

The town mouse and the country mouse
sat down to eat a dinner of barleycorn and
roots. The town mouse tried a few nibbles but
he did not like the dinner and he did not like
the country.

At last the town mouse said,
"The country is dull. My poor friend, you
only eat roots and corn. You should see how I
live! You must come to my house in town."

The country mouse had heard exciting tales
about town life and the wonderful food to be
found there.

The country mouse said, "Thank you for
your invitation. I would enjoy the town for a
change."

So the town mouse and the country mouse
went to town.

The country mouse had never seen so many houses before. They hurried past many fine buildings until they came to the largest house in the street.

"This is my house," said the town mouse proudly.

The town mouse took his friend into the larder. The country mouse saw at once that there was plenty of food in the house. He had never seen anything like it. There was cheese and honey, figs and apples, nuts and dates.

"This is better than barleycorn and roots,"
thought the country mouse.

The town mouse and the country mouse sat
down to dinner. The country mouse was very
hungry and he reached out for a piece of cheese.

Just then a man came in. He was carrying a broom and he was about to sweep up the food when he saw the two mice.

He shouted out: "Rover! There are some mice in this larder! Come on, boy! Catch them!"

The town mouse and the country mouse
ran off to hide in a hole. What a huge man!
What a nasty lot of noise! The town mouse
and the country mouse kept as quiet as mice
in their hole. It was dark and cramped but at
least it was safe.

When the house was silent again, they came out to eat their dinner. Luckily it was still there, and by now they were very hungry. The town mouse took some nuts and dates, and the country mouse helped himself to cheese and apple.

Then they saw a dog. Its big wet nose came
sniffing round the door. It was Rover! He had
come to catch them!

The town mouse and the country mouse
were frightened and lost their appetites at
once. So they ran off to hide again.

Poor country mouse! Every time he started eating, someone came along to frighten him away. He could not eat his dinner and he did not like the town.

The town mouse and the country mouse waited until the house was quiet again, and then crept out of the hole.

The country mouse decided that he would go home.

"My good friend," said the country mouse, "so much happens in this town. You have lots of food but you can never eat it in peace! There are men and dogs coming and going all the time. This town is too exciting for me! I shall be on my way."

The country mouse ran all the way back home.

There was his comfortable ditch, and there was the peaceful countryside all around him. He had a meal of barleycorn and roots, and then lay down to rest.

"I may be poor and dull, but at least I can live here in peace," he said happily.

The Farmer and
His Sons

An old farmer worked hard all his life.
He grew big, juicy grapes in his vineyard.
They were big and juicy because the old man
worked so hard, digging and forking and hoeing
carefully around every vine.

When the grapes were ripe, he sold them at the market. People paid a lot of money for such juicy grapes.

But the old farmer was not happy. He was a very worried man.

The old farmer had three sons. They were all very lazy. They never did any work, not a scrap. They had no idea how important it is to work hard.

The three sons just lay in the shade all day, leaving all the work to their father. The old farmer wanted his sons to do well. He wanted to teach them how to be good farmers.

So one day the farmer said, "There is a great treasure in my vineyard. Remember that when I die." It was enough to talk about treasure, the old man thought.

He saw how interested his sons were. If he had told them about hard work they would not have been interested at all.

When the old farmer died, his sons
remembered what he had said. Of course they
remembered! There was hidden treasure in the
vineyard. They were very excited. They thought
about bags of gold, sacks of coins and chests
bulging with silver and pearls.

All they had to do was dig for it.
"Let us find the treasure!" they cried, and
ran out into the vineyard. They set to work
immediately with spade, hoe and fork.

They dug hard and looked all over the vineyard for the treasure. They hoed out the weeds in case the pearls were hidden under them. They turned over the hard soil with their forks looking for gold and coins.

They dug deep with their spades in the hope
of finding a bulging treasure chest. And they
carried on digging, week after week.

They worked very hard for a long time, but not a penny could they find. Not a single pearl or a nugget of gold. Absolutely nothing! And they had worked over every bit of the vineyard.

"Father must have been playing a trick on us," they said. "There is certainly no treasure in this vineyard."

So they gave up work and just lay in the shade. They were very disappointed.

But by now the vineyard was so well dug
that the grapes soon grew big and juicy. It was
a dry, bad season for other farmers, but not for
the three sons.

Their grapes were better than any that had
ever been grown before.

When the grapes were ripe, the sons took
them to the town to sell in the market.

Everybody crowded round to see such
marvellous grapes. They all wanted to buy
some. People paid a lot of money for the grapes
at the market.

In a short while, the sons sold all the grapes
and their pockets were full of money.

The sons were amazed. "The grapes are the treasure from the vineyard," they said. "Hard work will bring us treasure."

Their father was right after all. He had taught them how to be good farmers, and they have worked hard in the vineyard ever since.

The Ass in the
Lion's Skin

An ass found a lion's skin one day. He stopped and stared. He sniffed and prodded it, until he was quite sure there was no lion inside it. Then he had an idea.

"I am not brave, and I never frighten people, even though I have a loud voice," he said. "If I put this skin on, people will think that I am a lion and the bravest and strongest animal in the whole wide world."

So he took the lion's skin and dressed up in it.

And there he stood, looking just like a lion. His nose and ears still stuck out of the skin a bit and so did his tail. But he felt like a lion. Soon he began to think that he was a lion.

He had heard that people were more afraid of lions than of any other animal in the whole world. So to prove it he went down to the village. What a brave ass!

The people in the village were going about
their business when one of them noticed an odd
creature trotting towards them.

"Surely not…" he muttered, and rubbed
his eyes. He looked again. "It is! It's a lion!" he
shouted. "Run for your lives, everyone!"

The villagers saw him coming and they ran
away. Helter-skelter they ran, and the ass ran
after them – *clippety-clop*.

"Help!" wailed the people. "We shall be
eaten alive!" And they ran faster and faster.

"What fun!" thought the ass, kicking his
legs high in the air. "The people are afraid
of me!"

The ass ran after them, but the lion's skin fell off. In his excitement the ass did not notice and ran on.

To frighten the people even more, he gave a mighty lion's roar: HEE-HAW!

Hearing this the people stopped and looked back. They saw that it was not a lion chasing them at all.

"Look! He is only an ass!" they said angrily.
"Fancy an ass daring to chase us! Let's chase
him back." So they ran towards the ass,
shaking their fists.

Without his lion's skin no one was afraid of the ass any more.

The ass saw the people coming and he ran away, because without his lion's skin he had no lion's courage.

What a silly ass!